RITA WONG

o
n
k
e
y
p
u
z
z
l
e

p o e m s

PRESS GANG PUBLISHERS
VANCOUVER

The Publisher acknowledges financial assistance from the Book Publishing Industry Development Program of the Department of Canadian Heritage, the Cultural Services Branch, Province of British Columbia and the Canada Council for the Arts. The publication of this book was also assisted by the Asian Canadian Writers' Workshop.

CANADIAN CATALOGUING IN PUBLICATION DATA

Wong, Rita, 1968–

monkeypuzzle

Poems.

ISBN 0-88974-088-7

1. Asian Canadians—Poetry* I. Title

PS8585.05975M66 1998   C811'.54   C98-910611-x

PR9199.3.W558M66 1998

Earlier versions of some works have previously appeared in the following journals: *absinthe* 8, *Fireweed* 36, *Contemporary Verse 2* (14.3 and 19.1), *Prairie Fire* 18.4, *Secrets from the Orange Couch* 3.1, *Tessera* 22, *West Coast Line* (28 and 31.2). Poems have also appeared in the anthology *Another Way to Dance*, edited by Cyril Dabydeen (TSAR Press, 1996) and *Millenium Messages*, edited by Kenda Gee and Wei Wong (ACWWS, 1998).

Edited by Claire Harris

Design by Val Speidel

Cover photographs by Chick Rice © 1998

Typeset in Filosofia

Printed and bound in Canada by Webcom

Printed on acid-free paper ∞

Press Gang Publishers

1723 Grant Street

Vancouver, B.C. V5L 2Y6 Canada

Dedicated to peace, love and justice

acknowledgements

My thanks to those who have supported and encouraged me:
Canace Wong, Peter Wong, Cindy Wong, Patrick Wong, Michelle
Sylliboy, Hiromi Goto, Susanda Yee, Yva Trout-Tail, Smoky, Lily
Shinde, Larissa Lai, Ashok Mathur, SKY Lee, Aaron Spitzer, Denise
Tom, Steven Lee and many more. Bouquets to Claire Harris and
Lydia Kwa for their sharp eyes and careful readings; Michelle
McGeough, Judy Lee and Tamai Kobayashi for the visual input;
Madeleine Thien, Della McCreary, Barbara Kuhne, Ann Macklem and
Val Speidel at Press Gang Publishers for their hard work. Some of the
communities who have sustained me: the Women of Colour Collective
and the Minquon Panchayat in Calgary, the Alberta/NWT Network of
Immigrant Women, *Kinesis*, Monsoon, the Vancouver Association of
Chinese Canadians, the No! to APEC Coalition, and of course the Asian
Canadian Writers' Workshop, especially Jim Wong-Chu. Good health
and happiness to you all.

This manuscript was made possible with the support of the Canada
Council Literary Arts Development Program, the Writers' Union of
Canada Mentorship Program (funded by Human Resources Develop-
ment Canada, Cultural Human Resources Council) and the Asian
Canadian Writers' Workshop 1997 Emerging Writer Award for Poetry.

contents

TRANSIDUAL

PASSION RAMPANT

IN SMALL SECRET ROOMS

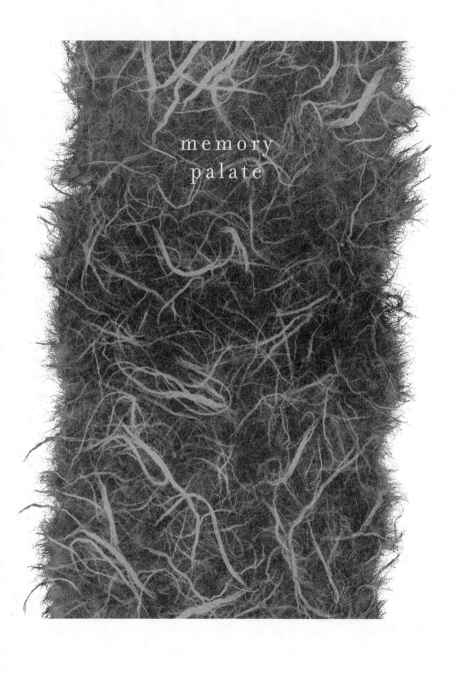

memory
palate

sunset grocery

at eight years old the cash register's metallic rhythm comes quick to
my fingers: 59¢ from $1.00 gets you back one penny, one nickel, one
dime, one quarter. could do this backwards in my sleep, & probably
have, but i prefer stocking shelves. prefer to avoid customers making
snotty fake chinese accents, avoid men flipping through porn.
open nine to nine seven days a week, the store is where i develop
the expected math skills: $60 net one day divided by
twelve hours is $5 an hour, divided by two people is
$2.50 an hour, or divided by five
people $1.00 an hour.

occupied with small details, sunset grocery can be duller
than counting the 20,000 times i breathe each day. i sell
cigarettes i am not allowed to smoke: player's light,
export a, du maurier. nicotine variations, drum &
old port. popsicles, twinkies, two percent milk. 7-up,
coffee crisp, bottles of coke. faced with these cancer- &
cavity-inducing goods, i retreat into books. by grade four
i learn the word "inscrutable" & practice being so
behind the cash register. however, i soon realize that i
am read as inscrutable by many customers with absolutely
no effort on my part, so i don't bother trying any more.

ten years of this means you can one day leave when
someone takes your place. what changes?

a skinny hallway connects three bedrooms in the back. i share
a room with my sister. our dog Smoky often sleeps by the bunk bed.
she snores. my sister talks in her sleep. down the hall
my father snores too. some nights, it's hard to tell
who snores louder—the dog or my dad. the nights are
noisy with all the things never said in the day.

the summer that i am afraid of fire, i hold Smoky every night
until the fear subsides. until my heart slows enough that i can
sleep. her stinky breath comforts me, reminds me of the many senses
we have to discover fire before it finds us.

the summer that i am afraid of fire, i always have a glass of
water near my bed. not enough to put out flames, i can at least
drink when i awaken, throat dry, sweaty & fearful in the night.

maybe because i am a fire girl, sparked between my parents' loins in
more romantic times, i know the power of fire, how it creates heat in
cold prairie winters, how it simmers, boils & stirfries countless meals
in the steaming kitchen, how it rests hungry within me, waiting for the

tinder of another body. the fear stems from fire's power to destroy,
to erase an existence eked out from penny nickel dime tedium.
to consume in minutes what took years to build.

one ear always attuned to the bell of the opening door i find i can't
trust or tell a straight story. what if flamboyant prometheus had been
an archer shooting down suns instead of bearing fire into human
hands? i draw witches with pointy hats & greenblack hair, dragon
ladies in salem garb, learn of ancient chinese secrets from american
laundry soap commercials. between amazons, milwaukee factory girls,
flying nuns, customers come in, customers go out. rabbits, cheese,
women populate the moon. flamethrowers light the sky with
their arms' circular logic.

part fire, part water, part air & part earth, i try to distance myself from
the fire within, fear that i cannot control its random blasts. i learn
to cultivate that part of me which is earth, sowing gradual seeds of
pragmatism, small quiet sprouts in the spring, studious endeavours
reaping scholarly harvests, parental approval,
respectable tunnels for escape.

as months grow into years, the fears go undercover, as do the dreams.
the connection between night & day is too painful
& so each morning i cross the river of waking washed clean of
nocturnal memory. the price for a respectable daytime existence is
high. it is my own desire. creating a vacuum,
the hollow space which i become.

when i return to the grocery store years later, that long echoing
childhood hallway seems dark, crowded, needing new carpet,
clean linoleum, anything to open it up, clear it of
so many night words still unheard.

the jade lady

the jade lady has dirty cracked fingernails. she is short, solid, bulky
with street-hawker attitude. before she came to canada, you would
have seen her squatting by the curb, wearing her ragged padded cotton
jacket, smoking a filterless cigarette, yelling *sen seen bok choy, ho
peng ah*! now she wears a padded silk jacket & sells jade every weekend
at the crossroads flea market. i have never seen her three sons, just
heard that they are good-for-nothing boys who never visit their
prune-faced mother. she has the eyes of someone who has been beaten
often & who has learned to hit rather than be hit, someone who pays a
penny less than the goods are worth, who counts every deal in the
blink of a cynical eye. her don't-mess-with-me eyes belie her frizzy,
artificially black, old-lady hairstyle. mom says to stay away from her,
even though mom gossips with her & buys jade from her. i can tell that
the jade lady thinks my mom is soft. & it's true that my mom always
pays just a little too much, isn't streetsmart enough to earn the jade
lady's respect. i have enough of my mother in me to know that i'm not
ready to haggle with the jade lady just yet.

crush

it was the eighties: i was wearing blue eye shadow, carrying a pouchy
headbanger purse with a rabbit's foot dangling off one end, & listening
to ac/dc. those of you who remember those days are probably groaning.
i remember being offered a joint in phys ed class, which i politely
refused. caught between wannabe bad girl & good chinese girl, i
usually chose the safe route. fitting into the times, the school, the
neighbourhood meant looking like a dopehead, but i was too well-
trained to act like one. meant ignoring the boy by my locker, the one
i had a crush on, when he turned to the girls beside him & said
something about a chink. the same boy i had once played tag with in
elementary was now an expert in adolescent cruelty & there was
nothing i could do. i think he's an accountant now. i hope he's
gotten over the cruel stage. i know i got over him that day.

headless buddhas
in a grassy field

the dead are still with us
sitting in chairs by our candlelit tables
jostling us in our sleepwarm beds

four in the morning dream stupor
i stumble to the washroom
where murky *toisan* village rivers gush
from between my legs, huts along the side,
farmers, rice paddies, barges float in
my waking dreams

where does ancestral memory end
& dream begin? i sleep
in cloudy territories of crowded ghosts
awaken with *teen ping chun, tun tem lay*
dissipating from my nostrils
kin apparitions evaporating
into the cool morning air

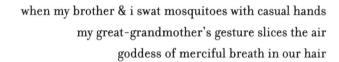

they live in the flicker of candle flames
the reflection we don't think we saw
plants that live no matter how we ignore them
shadows of flying birds
clatter of utensils against dishes as we wolf down our food
shudders of famine reverberating one generation to another

when my brother & i swat mosquitoes with casual hands
my great-grandmother's gesture slices the air
goddess of merciful breath in our hair

beware the mountain tigers

don't go near that open window at night
wild tigers might eat you

so ting ting (not yet a mother)
lay on the bed sweating & waiting for poh poh
to finish her mahjong game

pung! their voices, distant opera, reassured
as she stared at the dark   looked for fire eyes & fangs
ignored the hunger gnaw   tried to think

of poh poh steaming dumplings
fresh-squeezed soya milk for breakfast
the characters she'd memorized

class tomorrow: twenty words to know, think, twelve strokes,
a hook, a swirl, but strokes turn into eyes into teeth
into a girl in the stomach of a tiger

too hot to close the window even if she dared go near it

clickety-clack clickety-clack a railroad
mahjong tiles collide two strokes three into the morning

memory palate

sleepy red moments
mutter skeletal
warped driftwood gathered
from beached languages

this bittersweet taste:
words we no longer have
replaced by ones we no longer want

the roof of my mouth hard
with the sound of the mundane
been goh sigh jeng jeen?
been goh poh chong?
whose labour counts?

always on the way to
vulnerable exits, hopeful entrances
memory hopscotches on the hardwood floor
whispers of forgotten aunts
daylight plays tricks
once you sang the rug's hieroglyphs
once you shut the doors tight
now the wind blows them wide

for kwong lee taitai, who landed in victoria
the year of the monkey, 1860

so much has changed so

little has changed

between you & me:

mobbings

occasional riots

the usual sneers*

chinese exclusion act

gold rush

attempts to put us

in separate schools

finally the right to vote in 1947

now head taxes apply[†]

to all immigrants

not just

us

---

* 1887: "Chinese [girls] ... as young as six years old are brought to B.C. for Chinese workers and 'white pleasure seekers.' Up to six 'crib prostitutes' live in 12 × 14 foot slatted crates in Vancouver's Chinatown. Exposed to the elements year-round, and ravaged by disease, physical abuse and starvation, many will die before they turn 13." (City of Vancouver Archives)

† From 1885 to 1923, Chinese immigrants were the only people charged a head tax to enter Canada. Due to this racist policy, the Canadian government collected about 23 million dollars from 81,000 Chinese immigrants. This money has never been returned to its rightful owners. Today, Canada discriminates against poor people by requiring immigrants to pay a so-called landing fee.

i found you
a merchant's wife
officially romanized
briefly mentioned in
that oppressive newspaper
The Colonist

one of many
silences i want to hear

for annie

China Annie of Idaho: ... one of the few who succeeded in running away
from her owner. belonged to a member of the Yeung Wo Co., escaped to
Boise to marry her lover Ah Guan. her owner charged her with grand
larceny for stealing herself, & after a four week search, she was
apprehended & taken to court. the judge, sympathetic to her cause,
dismissed the case & allowed her to return to her husband.

—Judy Yung, *Chinese Women of America: A Pictorial History*

i.

i am not annie, i am of annie & i want it back. my eyes, my lips, my
fingers, my breasts, my rumbling stomach. all mine. my blood
thundering to deafen an army. jab of my insistent elbow. my pulse
beats defiance: i am i am.

ii.

our laughter, our secrets, even these were betrayed in the end.

so now i am a thief. funny how i always knew i'd be
a scarlet woman, lucky red, flaming alive. my signals
can be picked up miles away. my sister & i used to play
at being two of the four chinese beauties, *xishi, wang zhaojun.*
we knew someday we'd find the other two. a continent separates us
now, & i am one chinese beauty left rebellious & stranded.
new borders i could never have predicted.

marry my own kind, i am told. a chinese man beat me sullen. another
chinese man helped me escape, massaged my tired back, kissed
smooth my neck's scars. what if it had been a black man doing the
kissing, or a white man, as it was for polly? what if the town had
whispered: "sell-out, traitor, miscegeny?" guilt a luxury, blame a fraud.
we have always done what we needed to do. am i lucky insofar as i ran
chinese? purity is a myth. culture has its own comforts.

v.

velvet gloves are not enough.

vi.

the one that got away. she was almond grace, salty treasure. we talked
rivers, waves & oceans into the night, her strong black hair & mine
tangling into nets to catch stories. my mouth waters when i allow
myself to remember her cassia lilted laugh. in another lifetime we
could have built villages of women. today she lives mountains, rivers,
taboos away. clench & shiver, clench & shiver into silence. the taste of
her salt on my tongue.

vii.

i toil in my garden these days, alone but not lonely. the sun welcome
on my face, fresh moist soil a solace beneath my nails. i stay put,
planted in my space, & even this is pleasure. years of
breathing fear drained my joy in movement.
these days, a firm body is a strong & deliberate act.
let the heavens revolve around me for a change.

monkeypuzzle

write around the absence, she said, show
its existence
demonstrate
its contours
how it
tastes
where
its edges
fall hard
on my stuttering tongue, how its tones &
pictograms get flattened out by the
steamroller of the english language,

live
half-submerged
in the salty home of
my mother tongue,
shallows

this is
the sound of
my chinese tongue
whispering: nei tou
gnaw ma? *no*
tones can
survive this
alphabet

its etymology of
assimilation
tramples budding
memory into sawdusty
stereotypes, regimented capitals,
arrogant nouns & more nouns, punctuated
by subservient descriptors. grammar is the dust on the streets
waiting to be washed off by immigrant cleaners or blown into your eyes
by the wind. grammar is the invisible net in the air, holding your
words in place. grammar, like wealth, belongs in the hands of
the people who produce it.

你肚餓嗎?

pomegranate days

:seed one

sour explode, days in transit
perpetual compromise
not wanting to partake but unable not to

seasonal meanderings
take me in take me out of the uniformed order

brute digestion in fact
economic circumstances in fact

where myth girls cleave to cities of fact
where i might patch together
where grammar shapes raw meaning
where subordinate clauses holler for recognition

spend my days dizzy from bus rides
exhausted fumes on pedestrian streets

always unfinished
always in movement

:seed too

personal ghosts, of which there are too many
of which i am my own worst

split open papaya
small pearls spill out
wet signatures
visceral on fingers:

the woman she could have been
the woman she is
negotiation in her very breath
learning to expand
cool, moist spirit
spirals down her chest
to her pearly toes

lupine & mischievous
the imp in imperial
she rivers hungrily to the moon
flow & ebb, smooth consciousness

miss, missed, missing the boat
so she can swim
in the vessel of herself

:seed free

because the red tinfoil is shiny
because the glow is enough
because the traffic light changes & we can move on
forgetting the rules that bound our feet

isolation begets forgetting
collective memory so painful
i want to scratch & scratch
until memory bleeds me clean

:seed for you

once bit
the english apple
must be
chewed & chewed & chewed

jaw tired
bone weary
this language has become you
trips up the cantonese stairs

tumble years back down
fall out, thud upon thud
from jumping that ocean/
river sticks to skin

home is where your tongue wags
even chinglish sputters
subordinate means under:
a standard, a yawn
a gap, a flapping jaw
chews & chews

:seed five

bite your tongue
memory oozes out:
cause & effect, so clean

can i swear my mother tongue?
swear it down, swear it blue
monkeys swear in velvet smooth
not missing a swing from the boat
fresh off, i'll chew on compromise
until i learn to like its
tart red taste

:residual seed: sex

sow meet
sow plant
sow imprint

encode meaning & shudder
littoral stroke
green tentacle skin
would growth not be threat but spread
heartleaf root inside me

the chew
railroar of traintrack builders' bones
absent women the addendum
so: to go back
           to go forward
shuttle till the return fixes in
abundant blackhaired monkeyheads
reverberate
bone echo

crash ocean mountain graves
residential misgivings an understatement
hazard an occupation

radical means root
sharp seminal taste on tongue
radical mythology accommodate me
: gingerskinned sisters holler stories

a wandering daughter's grammar

she congregates with nomads
attentive & occasionally settling
reconjugates self with each meeting:
i am self
I is personae
i & stolen grammar
hoarded carefully in bare hands & forgotten pockets
aiya! hai been dou ah?
good fortune, she's a tough cookie
will bend & trace those words to follow black, black hair
the sound between her bare thighs as she walks & sidesteps
mimics & repels the roles imposed upon her

remember: timidity begets timidity
speak up, girl!

lip: to be used as a verb whenever possible—she lips backbone, a daily
necessity this slow road through thickets

tongue: caught between the command performance of communication
& her tongue's own slippery dance. thrust into the chasm of speak or
be spoken for.

哎
呀
！
係
邊
度
呀
？

breast: in conjunction with chicken evokes fear. in conjunction with
lover, a welling, a swelling, of touch & of shyness

knuckle: layers of work ethic, prone to cracks & dryness, punishment
in a harsh climate

back: her neural arch supports the clan's full frontal reunion,
genealogies writing themselves before her wary eyes

liver: proteins of endearment, this interrogative organ delivers feast
into fuel, water into blood

guilt: a way of life, can be slowly unset by the beating heart's optimism.
atriums of responsibility   a syntax of action.

sisterhood: this anatomy includes mother   if possible

prosopopeia

my projection. alter ego. myself. who is so removed, so absent. a
watcher. the page of cups. the thinker & silent worker, but preferably
not the talker. stains, shadows, imprints. the problem with being the
moon rather than the sun, the problem with being perceived as
dependent, when really, the moon exists however we choose to
interpret her.

the door is not locked, though stiff to open.

memory creeps slowly in, a gentle woman with orange oil-stained
fingers, childhood bruises beneath her cloak.

.

the games girlchildren played. skipping hopscotch tag murder ball
dodge ball. learned more complex games, continued playing even
when the names changed. dating. acting. motion. the sun on my skin
this morning, fresh dewy air: easily hopping, agile on sidewalks,
running on pavement.

.

motion calls. i listen.

.

red ribbon sneaks under the door, down the pockmarked sidewalk,
past frat houses, a church, a daycare, toward a solid brick house.
onslaught of dark & lack of curtains. i can see two people in the living
room, a pragmatic-looking asian woman & a bald white man. i would
like to imagine them arm-wrestling, but they are just sitting on a teal
chesterfield talking. their mouths flap in the lamplight, make them
magnetic in an artificial attractive, moving-picture way.

the problem of being perceived through confucius & the joy luck club.
is connie chung pragmatic-looking? the equation that connie does not
equal me does not equal suzy wong.

the door is not locked, though stiff to open.

.

i try not to stare at the muscles in her arms, breathe the soft smell that
announces her, pushes her into my imagination when i sleep.

.

fingers black with inkstone, my hands tremble in their calligraphic endeavour to be strong, firm, impressive. a betraying crookedness reveals itself on the rice paper, releasing my status as a foreigner to myself.

bold black characters pronounce *love, peace, freedom*—the desire but not the conviction of experience.

.

in this telling, my imaginary friend is a bald asian woman, strong in her transgressions & teal leggings. cheeky grin. bold eyes.

.

while cooking in the kitchen, her shadow stretches long & skinny, starts juggling fruit & doing the cancan. she is moving like a river with oceans to love, mythical coves to cleave to, sun on a jumping salmon's back. a quiet woman with her head bent over in concentration has a shadow capable of anything. watch her carefully before you walk into her home.

.

to set aside fancy tricks, cleverness, to strive for intelligence &
honesty, scares me, already so serious. i am drawn to elaborate nouns,
pomegranates, persimmons, speculum, iguanas, drawn to
the stranger taste on my tongue, this usage that uses me.

to come to terms with the quicksand that is "me." impossible.
herculean. give me a trite make-out scene on that chesterfield, let me
throw some fictional characters & places between me & you.

i am scared of saying something you will understand, stuck in a groove
where i want to reach out to you, yet drawing back in fear of actually
touching

pandora street

yellow crane shifts   floats heavy boxes across cement walls
magpies chatter messy wisdom   industry rumbles away
man on a bicycle: where's powell street?
i shrug, don't talk to arrogant voices   the city does that to me
boy disappears into a rented home   retinal haze obscures his face
graffiti makes it clear   women work   this street at night
rift of styx   doing tricks   along this curb
hope flutters on a girl's collarbone

alone in the playground i scribble   men drive by staring
don't see   their grimy light missiles   ballistic myths
target the first woman   who professes to share
her gifts with the ungrateful   they stone me for their sins

yet centuries of strong mothers bred me
blood crossing oceans & mountains
my cells shout history
my cunt throbs rivers of longing
my black hair invites a lover's pull
i'll debate you faster than i'll kiss you

meanwhile the western gaze frames
cardboard dolls in cardboard boxes
miss saigon's grandmother is spanking mad
suzy wong's aunties have had enough of this crap

i walk down the street   a lone asian woman   a loaded act
tender as gentians   subtle as spring
when the wannabe pimps come knocking
i'll be out dancing with the girls

puzzlinen

blood red dye #3
iron chink fish gutter
tins   rust

put into knit penguin purl two & woven baskets
strandmade   berry-dyed in woof cones weft china
thread proceeds to east timorese rebels
chinese students grassroots africville   doing
language slow consciousness juggle   fishgasp & leap
struggle with what   put your toe on   slid—
grasp for rail   de-railed   juggle jaguar grin bear
children & stories   maybe this that ribbon other or sprigs
on crazyquilt patch   sprigs on underwear before rip

fury channel
push

to oceans jump   to mountains track   over over over
not yet   to photographs tell   to trunk open over
only   laundromats always open   sundays even
punch the cash register over   cheap food
pull the door   it won't open   for you
what's wrong   you

everyone else	can
they don't see it	laugh
basket	chase
re	run
suzy wongs	pocahontas! run!
give them	hot food?
rotsa raffs	voice? what voice?
you must	make this up

down south peachwomen:
minimum wage pickers

calloused the gingerknobby
hands perform
broken willow baskets   the tongue stinging persimmon
plum kids out   of sore cherry wombs
squish   pomegranate seeds tart drops of
memory   traintrack over bigfooted bodies
chew chew chew that fruit
you wish but your job is to
pick the merchandise

can we catch a rhythm catch a train   c'mon can we
escape the pesticide curse
get paid what we are worth
pidgin women unite

       .

unite who? wudja mean by workers?
:listen: peachpickers hummm
one she picks, another she cans, another she cooks
it means rhubarb pie & more
       feasty days of noodles & rice & fish & tofu &
       pork & dumplings & chicken & bean soup;
sung in the kitchen. sung into existence, ya'd think.

sung & sweated & worried & wrung. dishcloth hung.
flat as a green onion pancake & even greasier.

you can do it: factory   kitchen   fields

reading my dinner

i listen to the city hum
its endless murmur of buses,
exploitation, crime & industry

as i eat
proteins gurgle
corporate betrayals
slide their way to
my stomach acids

difficult to nourish justice
on the supermarket shelves
every choice
a link in the faulty chain

a songbird warbles of food
on southern tables
the demilitarization of stock markets.
RRSP this!

there is every reason not to laugh
the newspaper a litany of reasons
not to laugh

only intuition at the back
of my throat says
a loose hand is faster
than a tight one
only laughing can i
survive the violence
of everyday transactions

frogs

hiding under my bed
purple frogs   blue frogs   ugly-as-dogs frogs
gay frogs come out of the closet
liberated frogs tickling my armpits my nostrils
wearing snazzy ribbons, berets,
hopping on the piano keys, tinkling out "chopsticks"
they chase cockroaches & dragonflies
form brotherhoods & sisterhoods with their pals the iguanas
norwegian frogs tibetan frogs arctic frogs in parkas
these frogs move too fast to ever get processed & glucose-covered
no these are hip frogs on the lookout for action

denim blues

there are denim mountains in my closet:
well-worn cutoffs, raggedy jeans,
adolescent skintight pants, baggy prairie overalls,
years of tacky stampede outfits

nothing comes between me &
the labour of the garment workers
their fifty cents a day sweat
hugs me tight every morning

my auntie's fingers nimble
with the demands of piecework
how she churns dozens of jeans by dim lamplight
one more casualty for casual wear

cotton picked by hungry workers
beaten into fabric & submission in far-off factories
dissembled into department store offerings

black denim with amputated
fingers waving bloody threads from pockets
knotting in my chest as i look in the closet
find nothing to wear

nothing, that is, but
thin faded gauze ripping open,
spilling labour into consumer vision,
ragged with guilt, ignorance, fear
but still rippling, a necessary banner
in the wind for change

periodic table

: sturdy calcium

drifting from your lactose-intolerant frame, particles forget to resist
gravity, bend your decades into cryptograms as you hobble down the
pungent chinatown streets, stopping to puff on a cigarette. you remind
me: toil, soya & fish heads, brush your teeth each night, a regime of
bitter herbs to strengthen the body's friction against time's slide.
aligning the orbitals of health.

: impervious zinc

sleeping tiger hills hide metals in their bowels. guarding against
corrosion & eczema, zinc's helical curves follow a rainbow arc. zinc's
cousin mercury a messenger of internal velocity, a sign that we were
never simple & pure. never.

: everyday neon

inert gas caught in the shape of a flying pig on hastings street. sour urine cloud hovers above bespittled, gum-encrusted sidewalks. this is the poorest urban neighbourhood in all of canada, a few blocks from the banks & the corporate bunkers. this is bars on windows, sad-smelling buses & survivors on streetcorners. we are only as successful as this, the city's lowest common denominator.

blood orange

where you expect familiar orange limbs
domestic workers, weary house cleaners,
bite into violent purple, congealed red surprise
reluctant juice

though we never asked to be
you make us your blood oranges—
be warned: our sangria circus days will end

blade abrupt
& flesh-weary of pin-up ardour
we can see ourselves through your eyes
this is how we have survived
ripening beyond your lids
to ferment revolution

no glossy pedestals for us
we will not settle for less than
salty justice, sharp honesty

while our sisters rot in sweatshops
we cannot sit in crimson pouts
for your prurient, near-sighted eyes

our spirits roar louder than your dollar
& can't be bought at penny-scratched magazine counters
you see a catalogue of lives for sale
we see each other's tears

you don't ever understand—
this is not about blood oranges in every supermarket
but the return of forests & rambling wild gardens
of nightwarm women yelling for our lives
tongues waging wars
faster than the flash
of your rusty silver knives

excerpts from
a diary of resistance

1. june 4, 1997

i drip wax on the sidewalk in front of the chinese consulate, deliberately leaving traces for people to find the next morning when they come out to drive their mercedes benzes. this is the eighth year since the tiananmen square massacre, & since i do not want to leave blood on the sidewalk, wax will have to do.

we walk up granville street, 300 strong, mostly chinese students my age, seniors, middle-aged couples, young parents carrying children in strollers or walking with them hand in hand, a woman six months pregnant, a few white people in solidarity with political prisoners. cars & taxis honk support every so often, one guy rolls down his window & yells "go home," someone shouts "we are," our placards & candles bob up, bob down, as we roll toward the consulate, each step weighted by the witness we bear to the young people slaughtered eight years ago.

what's a few hundred or even a few thousand people, you might ask, since we know that mass murder is not new in china or anywhere else. in canada i have just to say *smallpox blankets.* but today we gather without being gunned down by tanks & soldiers. i, who speak more english than chinese, have the privilege of standing around feeling sad for the dead, bored when i don't understand the speeches, cheered by

tipping a flame to a little boy so he can light his own candle, sheepish
when we find shelter under a tree because of the rain. going about
mundanely. despite cameras trained on us by the chinese consulate.
despite canadian police guarding the consulate's gate.

if we were 3,000 instead of 300, would the state thugs attack? not guns
but pepper spray perhaps. not justice, not public safety. this is not
about democracy in china or in canada.

*democracy has become a myth ... when you know that multinational
corporations have more of a right to decide what happens to your world,
your environment, your life & your security than you do.*

this is not about democracy. look, democracy is plunging into the
sea burning up hissing at a million miles an hour. this is about
remembering.

---

* Jeannette Armstrong

a man yells out the names of students who are still in prison in china today, the roll call taking me back to a vigil last week in alexandra park. naming the people who have died of AIDS in vancouver this past year.

now again, we mourn by candles, mourn by tears, mourn by these stubborn human gatherings.

2. *july 1, 1997*

london newspaper headline: "they didn't even say thank you!"
who said they were ever welcome?

hong kong's ghost rises in a blown out candle's strand of smoke, a
noisily starting car's blue exhaust, a boiling pot of red bean soup's
steam. hong kong's ghost is fleshly bustle, can gamble with the
practiced ease of someone who's done it for centuries, who's still
doing this, the big gamble. whether mother slaps you or gives you
an orange to eat, she is still mother. mother holding a big gun &
heavy tomes of history. public face & private plans, mother's strings
pulled by rich old men. coins falling from her cleavage as she bends
toward you.

during the changeover ceremony, as prince charles & chris patten
board the yacht to leave hong kong, my aunt sits in her living room,
half watching the british imperialists depart, half flipping through
hong kong pop culture magazines & scratching her nose. in tiny
apartments everywhere, people sit, scratching & waiting.

3. november 1997

for the delta force five & cupe 454

november is pepper spray in students' faces, remembering first
nations soldiers who fought in world war II only to be denied veteran
rights in canada, the rain that falls & falls, november is the cruelest
month as dictators dine in vancouver on taxpayer dollars, as the media
erases political prisoners like leonard peltier & mumia abu jamal one
more year, as i shiver on the picket line witnessing the decay of
workers' rights & learn the value of a thermos when we are locked out,
as men who have fallen out of the crumbling education system break
into another car, as another friend dies of AIDS, november is the
cruelest month, the month that kills any poem's right to live, as
everything keeps falling down & picking itself up again, the month
when all bets are off, the month when you learn that escape is an
illusion, events spiral into each other the way monkeypuzzle limbs
appear to spiral skyward as they curve toward the spinning earth, the
month of knowing what it means to be lied to. november is when i
yearn for where sand meets ocean but can only see alleyways. when the
act of imagination is all that keeps the soul from collapsing into itself.

grip

*A 10-year-old [Chinese Indonesian] girl returning from school discovered
that the shop and house where her family lived and worked had been
burned. As she went in search of her parents, she was seized by
two men and raped in front of her neighbours.*

—"Accounts of Gang Rape of Chinese Women Emerge from
Jakarta Riots," NEWSWIRE, MAY 1998.

her parents could not save her or the store. windows shattered, shelves
raided, drinks, canned goods, fruit, cigarettes, virginity all stolen.
blood, litter, dead bodies where her home used to be. walls smoking
black in jakarta.

as money flows back & forth between canada & indonesia, the
indonesian army stands around watching the rape. global economy,
global atrocity. men in suits have decided: scapegoat the vulnerable
while the real deals go down. the stupid rapists don't touch the
minister of finance no they rape an innocent girl a shopkeeper's
daughter who has no control over the price of rice soybeans cooking
oil eggs

the long history of terror for the chinese the jews the africans the east
timorese the tibetans. violence too familiar to the diasporic & the
indigenous. but this girl whose hair smells of her burnt home, the
childhood she will never have back, this is hers alone

transidual

this work is not about the third world. nor is it about colonialism.
it is about us in the first world & where & how we fail.

—LAIWAN

i was dreaming my geography
but it's time to wake up

i touched the tip of the mythical silk
road one afternoon as the bus
sputtered to our impoverished
destination. from one city of thieves to
a small village of thieves. "thieves"
trying to take back what was theirs in
the first place: dreams, camels, stars,
words. ghosts of traders stared
uncomprehendingly at my blank face.
centuries of barter echoed in the air
between us. this place not merely the
route of imperial extravagances but also
a dusty path of peddlers, two faces of
the same heavy coin.

the coin sits cool on my palm.

a merchant's daughter raised on a
practical diet counting change day in
day out, i can smell how money snakes
along the city road, only occasionally
meandering to leak a few coins into the
surrounding countryside.

i exchange coins: this is the tainted
way of tourists. silk roads lead to cave
paintings. paved roads lead to suit &
tie clad moneycharmers. dust particles
are everywhere, each one holding
someone's memories. the stench of
some memories is too strong to breathe.
can't bear to inhale the thickskinned
tourists around me as they bargain for
goods they can easily afford. tourists
who take photographs of hungry
children. particles hang in the light,
these waves we call history.

chinese & not chinese

when i start gushing about crowds stinky trains monkeys for sale lamb
dinners in yurts caves in luoyang terra cotta soldiers & holy
mountains, distortion sneaks in, making them "exotic" or "other,"
when what i want to say is that they're visceral, real. these places are
not foreign to those who live them.

the adventure, for me, is not to gawk at the people, whose skin & hair
call me home, but to navigate these streets an independent woman. a
woman uneasily negotiating the currency of foreign birth.* a woman
who sees how being "chinese" houses both pride & shame under the
same roof.

i remember a nine-hour bus trip through gansu province, western
china's dust bowl. people stubbornly & miraculously survive among
these raw parched sienna cliffs. the ride vigorous as we bump & rattle
toward xiahe, home of a tibetan monastery. denise & i hunch over the
hard seats, trying to bounce with the bus. across the aisle, a chinese
woman is barfing yet again, & i want to offer her a gravol except i'm
shy. she's stopped again, & maybe this time she will last the next few
hours. all this time, she has been vomiting into a small plastic bag, &

---

* "The structure I hate also hates me, but it makes me, and that's where the problem starts."
—Jeff Derksen

when the bus driver stops for a pee break, she asks the guy beside her to throw the bag out the window. the look on his face as she hands him the bag of vomit still makes me roar with laughter. in fact, the woman starts laughing, & denise & i start laughing, & pretty soon, even the guy with the bag is howling.

when we finally get to xiahe, there are dogs roaming the dusty streets, & hundreds, no thousands of monks everywhere. young prepubescent monks playing pranks on each other, old fat monks, big athletic-looking monks running after carts, hungry monks gobbling noodles in the restaurants, & even a few nuns wandering about.

the dust blows & blows, & i need to spit, which is so common here that no one thinks twice of it. having acclimatized, i figure i can do it just like anyone else in the crowd. however, i forget to consider the wind factor. sure enough, the glob ends up on my shoes instead of on the ground, & my friend is howling loud enough to outshout the gusts of wind pushing us about. a quick look around the street: did anyone else see? reassured that no one cares, i start laughing too.

denise & i are both chinese canadian but only blend in when people
are unobservant, exhausted or just plain innocent. i can't count the
number of times that we've been asked "are you japanese?"
sometimes, we try to pass, to quietly sneak by as possibly chinese from
some other part of china, modernized shenzhen or guangzhou—just
one generation removed from truth. as my chinese improves, it
becomes increasingly feasible to imagine this role, indeed tempting to
grow into it.[*]

but here in this little wind-dried town, we are clearly foreigners with
big backpacks. moreover, we are tourists: who else would come here?
the monks, we find, are friendly for the most part. we chat with some
young monks who are cute in that austere muscular way, monks who
sing raunchy songs, monks who incidentally give us the fire in the
belly to go to tibet.

& how i want to go to tibet. how i dream of countless jigsaw poses of
tantric figures, sipping yak milk tea, vultures circling human flesh for
the sky burial, even altitude sickness. at the same time, how i fear the

---

* "There is no real me to return to." —TRINH T. MINH-HA
  The *to* in story no final destination.

chinese army's brutality, fear the ever present threat of guns, fear how the labour gangs & prisons outnumber the monasteries.

chinese & not chinese, i hate what my beloved china is doing to tibet. how a million tibetans have died under this occupation over the decades, how their homeless roam, settling in pockets around the world, to wait, to pray, to remember. how millions of chinese are denied truth, hearing of economic progress but nothing of genocide. how i would gladly give up my own dreams of going to tibet if those forced to leave could return to their homeland. how the devout walk the high, arid plateau of this world as witness.

lips shape yangtze,
chang jiang, river longing

three gorges, you whisper
the sound of rocks filling your mouth:
we, who have always been displaced by poverty,
sent across the ocean to find rice

i look for the big sky
but clouds suffocate me
rain defeat for the dispossessed.
families pushed out of homes,
mouths gaping hunger.
stone soup, stone face,
cracking as earth reveals herself through us

throat.   gorges.   the glottal stop rising into my nose
pressure on my lungs one hair away from unbearable
the heaviness: signing the dotted line
when you cannot read what you've signed

without memory, we die fast & brutal
flooded by greed
our drowned, bloated arms wave
and who will wave back?

the sound of rock breath
falls empty onto diasporic spray
light wet on black hair

we miss the boat, even as we disembark

rat traps

       & the hesitation of opening doors
should the rat scamper free

anonymous prowls around town
into this cacophony of smells
eggrot freshblacktractorexhaust stalegarlicsweat
charredshishkebabs & the comfort of apples
as she walks she revels in the ease of women
a touch a firm hold guiding her tactfully through
to dodge the donkey shit frozen spit human mules on the road

through the deluge anonymous   retreats to   shelter
what more real & therefore safe than the central room in our house
that stinking bathroom, not all the incense in china could purge it
she holds her breath. look, don't smell:
       two washstands at attention
       scantily clad with facecloths
       basins flipped to dry
       a diagonal semaphore waiting
       invisible stench waiting
       mud soap waiting
       temperamental heater waiting
for the next meeting of electricity & water

the beauty of an empty centre, not here
here the beauty of chaos disperses, black hairs shedding
into barely perceptible question marks, thin as the whistle
of the midnight train

drifting through random cock crows & donkey moans she
is once again slapped from functionally safe into
startlingly alive
anonymous can consider guerrilla tactics at this point:

hit & leave in the night

the terror of performance

personal starvations

when i take the pool cue

when i aim for the hard little ball & miss
when math & body meet
but coordination can't make it
when it is dark streetside
smalltown in shandong province
when it is so heavy humid
when i am in that testosterone space, the pool table
when older men kindly tell me
hold it this way
change your fingers
bend lower   concentrate
when i smile polite thanks & then proceed
to hold the stick my way
when i know i will lose this game, their game
but i will do it my way
when my chinese-from-china friend asks
"do they have pool in canada?"
when i grit & nod yes,
tempted to lie, no, that is why i
can't play worth beans
when someone is silently counting the score
& i disregard them
when we are looking for something to do

when i am going to blend in or shock without effort
when the night is so guarded & red
when i drop the words i don't want
when i practice deliberate amnesia, survival tactics
when i implicate myself in imperialism
by ignoring the score

hello, china

hey, look, how i fit into the crowd
just another black-haired woman on a bustling market road
just another woman on a bicycle
and my bicycle is rusting, squeaking, complaining
that i'm going too fast
that there are too many bikes on the road
that the brakes are tired.
i'm used to it now
just ride along
business-as-usual
till a puddle smacks me
and i slide
into the cement
with the smooth speed of oil on a road
blood to show where my face meets cement
mud to show where my elbow meets ground
hello, china, i'm here now
i read you
taste your dirt ingrained into my split lip
wear your embrace around my bruised eye
your marks fade from my skin in a few weeks
leaving me your long-tongued kiss

string me a line ...

we take a three-hour train ride
to the kite festival
only to find that it ended last week

still, we head to the kite museum
salvage the journey
with the efficiency instilled by our parents
acrobatic poses, cicada rustles, the inevitable dragon
myths & legends flattened onto paper
to float against the unsuspecting sky

a few sticks   thin rice paper   some string:
let the construction begin

weeks later, my friend's seven-year-old daughter
knocks on my door with innocent face
asks me to help fly her kite
my best attempts drag along the ground
hop skip & fall

pedestals shift & collide
wind blowing them off their fragile strings
into the polluted sky
gaudy bold red
like the colour of memory & unspoken trysts

would the emperor's kite have six claws?
would the demons of this world please raise their hands?
would string slice the dancing pig
turn pastime into sustenance
story into food?

my hands ache to let go

for the pig

the pig pissing
the pig enclosed in a wicker basket its size
the pig cannot move a leg cannot fight its coming slaughter
the pig on the back of the bicycle in a wicker basket
the pig & the sunlight
the sunlight hits the stream of piss
at just the right moment
just the right angle
turning it golden with the colour
of the pig's protest
an elegant trajectory
of the pig's fear

me on another bicycle
a few feet away
with just enough time
to swerve
to see with camera's eye
the beauty of the pig pissing
its last word

passion rampant
in small secret
rooms

in the teasing of
a cellular dream

bones. capillaries. limpid fluids. one cell of meaning in the marrow,

soft, pillowing bone splinters spindling a hardening past, empty

seesaw teeters in a familiar playground, wind through leaves in my

head, rustling into a wider self. words slip globular through veins,

arteries, slow down at joints, pulse faster in heated lovemaking.

dead words, forgotten phrases, gather in fine hairs on my arms & legs.

dead sentences sprout black & downy on endlessly regenerating skin.

these words had power once & could have power again, hence let

no one have your hair or nails, let no one steal your body's words,

let no one rein the loose heart of your present. the ankle of the

moment supports a whole body of work, snaps if attacked from a

vulnerable angle. let your ankles be naked in the face of fear, follow

the wind's clues yet bear steady in changing currents. the curve of

slim muscle remains a wondrous act.

warn the town, the beast is loose

—THE FUGEES

and the naming of the intolerable is itself the hope

—JOHN BERGER

let me dive into this winedark sea, be the vessel of your allusions. synecdoches of ancestors, metonymies of desire, metaphors of justice. survival's rhetoric bears down on this dancing puppet hand. what keeps this sentence-stringing creature from madness? only the pretense of response, meridians of words aligning themselves between us. episodes of exchange, barter me an eye for an ear, a liver for a gall bladder, sweaty palms for rosy cheeks. only a monsoon alert: a flock, a pack, a rage of dykes on the loose. a flood, a collective, a gang of two-spirited women. only the naming saves the namer. only as honest as the telephone wires carrying these words to you. snapping in storm, swaying in wind, a taut line of chestache for birds to perch upon. currents & fiery threats hidden beneath the windswept grass.

a good spy is but the secret writer of all moments imminent

—CHANG RAE LEE

virginia, this is what I would say to you if we were standing together on granville island:

stink of a sailor's fart the drift of ocean carried by wind into my nostrils the colour of seasmell is green mud, light, translucent mud, line of beach & sky, the mirror of waters meeting & always the sea waves lap the dull unending rhythm waters jostling, rolling, moving in perpetuum & the smell, the smell reminds me, reminds me of what is at the other side of the ocean, photographs of time travelling, the boat anchors me, seagulls poop all over cement waterworn wood deck with gaps & the underbelly seasmell of the bridge, salty taste of fish & chips, oily slicker of a fisher's net, tangle of seaweed as it catches in my throat, as i swallow its salty soup, aftertaste of pork bones, seasmell forgotten as stinky travelsweat invades, boats & perfumed tourists, furtive gropings under the bridge nights before this crowded daytime market, the dark, lonely face of a girl in the shadows & an orange painted so well it looks like a photograph, sound of one hand slapping, endless feel of cool wet sea & sweat of birds, the sea, the sea, the sea, her sister the wind, & i am smelling her underbelly, invisible creatures trying to live in polluted water, birth of a thousand starfish, placenta floating on shore on a sunny day if the ocean roars will the women come? come to sing the high song of eating fish, greasy mermaids stuttering in the aftermath of a motorboat, the sister city of yokohama

we are & will that prevent war? the border of bridge, traffic, cement
working along up to the memory of another day & how it is not what i
say but how i continue to say it, because my monkey mind has been
well, well trained & i can't see the point of writing when so many other
urgent needs call, the sea beckons, other countries' faces hinted at the
horizon's brief slip alongside debris, flotsam, crushed shells wait out
the polluted wash of horn & trumpet seafarers cruiseship prison no
life for anyone the hard slug of sweaty fingers ambisexual we are

parchment

this globe my body so dry its surface flakes white, the only time this
skin is white. upon contact, your eyes on my skin write an old tale,
words we know too well. with time, we wrestle new stories from each
other, nets rip with each sweaty assertion. we are not all the same. the
trail of saliva leads here to your tribe & my tribe in this room private
as the histories in our stretched muscles. i mark you with my fingers,
my hair, my teeth. inscribe my body's anecdotes upon you so that you
cannot name me foreign. i speak myself against you, year after year,
replenish the oasis in this desert. you will learn my dialect as i have
learned yours, the pages of our exchange rustling anew. a pact,
you & i, a pact.

butterfly lovers

i. striped blue crow

antennae full of spring, the lightest breeze tells you, woman or man, blush of gender half stolen, azure sashay, *euploea mulciber*, your androgynous vowels steaming the air between us. you brushed against me, i knew phonetics of infatuation, gasp of an asian legend echoing in the long dark corridors like a tinny recording of that old opera.

ii. autumn leaf

you told me i smelled like autumn, & i will always remember those words floating out of your lips & into my chest. i am the song of death approaching before life returns, compost of tawny remnants, seasons of ripening genes. for you, i am perpetual departure.

iii. lemon emigrants

bursting from those little island countries, from that giant land mass we call asia, wombs full of little eggs, yolks waiting to spread into this white white land. *catopsilia pomona*, thank god for our invasion, they would have eaten one another if they didn't have us.

iv. white swordtail

like the bride with white hair, you cut a fearsome swath across my
path, can kill with one quick flick, your dainty edges a knife's dream.
kung fu fighting will never be the same. your acrobatics predate all
these white sifu-wannabes. i'll bow before your swift laugh.

v. cruiser

you didn't know it but i was cruising you across the room, the smoky
dance floor, trying to insinuate familiarity, as though my sweat had
graced your brow, your cut sleeve brushing my excited tips. may we fall
into one another, rain drops returning to the ocean?

vi. plain tiger

crouched in dark alleyways, we play crickets, hide & seek. they call us
gangs & we call them racists. they stop us at the border because they
fear our black stripes. they draw us with white spots on brown, black
spots on yellow, every time still although we are always in motion. i
cross these lines for you.

between you, me & the bedpost

this poem wears army boots
smells of fresh polish
doesn't gush   but speaks
cool silence between verses

this poem wears its brush cut &
black leather jacket
with casual swagger
has confident hands
& hides a soft belly
you'll only see in the bedroom

yessiree, this poem has morning breath
doesn't bathe every day
likes the smell of her stanzas
& tends to be moody

if you break up with her
she'll survive
what's more she'll still kick ass
she wants you to know this

when this poem looks at the big sky
the foggy streets, the rumpled bed
she tastes your smoke   feels you hot
against her naked words

passion rampant in small secret rooms

your big loud laugh
revives my starving ghosts
coaxes the peripheral slow slow into graceful centre
my flesh rising to your occasion

adrenaline memory insinuates
knuckles me awake
i am cartilage to your bone
hungry teeth to your tongue

sweet curds of temptation   fragile with promise
might evaporate if i stare too directly

but already your presence shifts planets
refracts me countless angles
toward my circling stars

disrupts the architecture of inheritance
blasts open the attic windows
you prove
a woman is her own house
dangerous & whole

mythology floes,
asian fleas

seeds of transcontinental drift, carried by volcanic ruptures
each risky metamorphosis hesitates
finger to the wind, testing

the gaudy music of our transgressions
now secret memories carried on the blink of a lash:
because i loved you, i left

our moment so full
it spilled me out

know you this:
you live in my dreams, the ones forgotten by daylight
you live unspoken in my everyday sentences
riding me like a shadow

i will always migrate toward love
ride the contradictory undertow
that leads me to leads me away from you

just one more love poem blossoming in a lilac spring

like a car going way past the speed limit
like an endless fall in dreams
like the osteopath's sudden wrench
like the most satisfying fart i've ever had
like a deep, succulent purple
like a waiting soldier's tilted head
like a long, slow cat stretch
like vines hugging a window
like a surprise ten-course banquet
like a rhythmic knee, thigh, hip stride on hot summer walks
like the milky pink pout of magnolias against dead branches
like the earth's crust shifting
like a foghorn at the opera
like an accidental computer virus
like the salty depths of my mother's seaweed soup
like the doggy tail wagging in the distance
like kissing was the national sport
like the catalyst in a chemistry lab explosion
like a wet tongue in a surprised ear
like amazons are for real
like the certainty of autumn
like food not bombs for everyone on earth
like hearing aretha franklin sing "Respect" live

like a kite escaping gravity

like revolution is an everyday word

like a mouthful of pomegranate squirt

like children playing tag in the streets

like knowing to hit water just keep walking a straight line

like a giant fern's primordial growl

like the persistent fungus in my neighbour's lawn

like elephants in heat

like when skyscrapers disappear leaving the sky naked

like a burning bush

like cannons exploding into tulips

like fire hydrants released

like child abuse forever stopped

like a plumber in my chest

like the heavy bend of branches holding too many blossoms

chloro fill

your deep fern
   drips, muggy spore
,waiting lips o ancient
     pulse sweaty
palms release stomach ,pit into
      rhythms green green ,o
   ,drip me ,drip you ,o
  humid now ,tug
     curving cell's throb
     throats into sigh
  o wonder o this ,ness
    ,torso us one
    full ,full
  fluid cry
    ,tumbling breath
head body skin ,body skin ,slow
  slow into blood

passionfruits, boy & goose*

in the middle is the bright red boy
carefully arranged around him:

7 pale green passionfruits

3 red-centred lotuses

the geese are hidden
look hard; there are 2 of them
behind this the green print patterns become 1 big leaf
carrying all these objects within its veins
boy geese fruits & flowers are specks on a leaf
tiny monkeys on some buddha's hand

    unlike momotaro who came out of the peach
    this boy never entered the fruit
    he just stands, angry red, surrounded by unripe fruit
    the geese hidden from his eyes
    he just stands, hungry

---

* Title of a painting by Hung Su Li.

seoul, 1989

il   liberation day. like the banks,
the canadian embassy is closed.
downtown: where are the student riots,
the tear gas. national museum closed
but department stores are open.

i   my penpal warns me not to hold hands with
another woman, the way men here hold each other,
or i'd be taken for a lesbian. i remember reading:
if i could choose my sexual orientation, i'd be gay.
would quote that but i'm not in the mood to debate.
he served in the military for a year.

sam   when i walked out of our *yogwan*
men were pissing in the alley.
didn't look shouldered through

sa   sound of cohen in subway shops.
purple corn. green & burgundy palaces.
squat toilets. hawkers in itaewon. cheap leather
expensive nightlife invisible women

o

take off, heroic couplet
flown to japan

shoulder roll into futon
firm cotton enveloping splat

only this white pillow, green leaf
and ladybug in the world

you are not supposed to be on this train
will they find you

hidden away in black hair
a back seat

still persimmon seeds
fall glossy onto the waiting earth

words come back rhythming
in a guava tint & hot day's promise

impaled on this elusive pivot:
them & me: who said that?

ricestacks through windows
mountaining through long trainride's bum-ache

punted out of one seat into another
you await detection

leavetaking

empty coathangers
clash. echo in the closet.
he will not return.

i walk with the spring
lightness of bare feet after
a winter of boots

:meeting implies purpose

—Erin Mouré

in san francisco county
four times as many asian women as asian men
married whites

where does the river of one race end
& the sea of another begin?

children leap oceans in their births
raised in new lands, carry silt in their genes
river offspring, shift deltas
tangential shades merge in twilight's blood

spontaneous burn & simmer
glow & kiss as candles tip together
before water & after it:
when a woman blossoms you into her
whose seed will history record?

because it is possible to decolonize
to recognize the aperture within opening
to feel change in your bones
i can carry the day forward once more

:I speak to you without election because the cells know nothing of
democracy.
They think not of the good of the whole, but of themselves.
They think of their thin unguarded border.

because the cells know hope
know the spiraling word's structure
know the touch of a stray cat
they can replenish in the night

when i squeeze the orange, pull it off the tree,
do the roots cry out? will the tree forget its pain?

:It must have to do with love, at its root.
No matter how it is obliterated after that

the relevance of salt water: our bodies
an ocean of immigrants' tears

---

* Italicized lines are from Erin Mouré, *Furious*.

my digestive stomach gurgle relevant
because it is the sound of the orange after the tree
& the sound of one pen writing
visible skin
furiously

furl of a rhubarb leaf
its red, red stem
the colour of the triangulation
in my chest: mothers,
daughters, holy ghosts

politics. with its trail of bodies.
seaslip. saltslick.
blood sticks.

s o m n i l o q u y

when a lover appears in your dreams with an ankle red-string-tied to yours, you will know this is the one. ripple on still waters hums electric pull. poesy of nightblack space, the ache you know better than yourself. opening sky as eyes adjust & clouds disband, revealing stars upon aching stars. flame of natural gas in the darkness, dancing curds of fiery light shooting from a slim metal pole. earth magic, enveloping the fields around us with a dim orange glow. song to my song, you are myrrh & incense, bread & roses. fireflies flitting an airy punctuation. in the grass together, we are home. tonight we have arrived.

Grateful acknowledgement is made for use of the following:

Judy Yung, *Chinese Women of America: A Pictorial History* (Seattle: University of
Washington, 1986)

Monty Python "Crunchy Frog Skit" in *The Golden Skits of Wing-Commander Muriel
Volestrangler FRHS and Bar* (London: Methuen, 1984)

Jeannette Armstrong, "Conference Proceedings of the Second International
Women's Conference Against APEC," Nov. 17–18, 1997, Vancouver, B.C.

"Accounts of Gang Rape of Chinese Women Emerge from Jakarta Riots," *Newswire*,
May 1998

Laiwan, *Distance of Distinct Vision* (Vancouver: Western Front, 1992)

Jeff Derksen, *Dwell* (Vancouver: Talon Books, 1994)

Trinh T. Minh-ha, *Woman Native Other* (Bloomington: Indiana University, 1989)

The Fugees, "The Beast," a song on the album *The Score*

John Berger, *And our faces, my heart, brief as photos* (New York: Pantheon Books,
1984)

Chang Rae Lee, *Native Speaker* (New York: Riverhead Books, 1995)

Hung Su Li, title of a painting reproduced in a Taipei Fine Arts Museum catalogue,
"Overseas Chinese Artists Exhibition," 1984

Erin Mouré, *Furious* (Toronto: Anansi Press, 1988)

Some resources and influences:

ASIA, the Asian Society for the Intervention of AIDS (http://www.asia.bc.ca)
Friends of the Lubicon (http://kafka.uvic.ca/~vipirg/SISIS/Lubicon/main.html)
Maquila Solidarity Network (http://www.web.net/~msn)
Multinational Monitor (http://www.essential.org/monitor/monitor.html)
Aquilar-San Juan, Karin, ed. *The State of Asian America: Activism and Resistance in the 1990's*. Boston: South End Press, 1994.
Anderson, S.E. and Medina, Tony, eds. *In Defense of Mumia*. New York: Writers and Readers Publishing, Inc., 1996.
Nozick, Marcia. *No Place Like Home: Building Sustainable Communities*. Ottawa: Canadian Council on Social Development, 1992.
Schumacher, E.F. *Small Is Beautiful: A Study of Economics As If People Mattered*. London: ABACUS, 1974.
Shiva, Vandana. Biopiracy: The Plunder of Nature & Knowledge. Toronto: Between the Lines, 1997.
Springer, Jane. *Listen to Us: The World's Working Children*. Toronto: Douglas & McIntyre, 1997.

RITA WONG grew up in Calgary and currently lives in Vancouver. She has taught English in China, Japan and Canada, and has worked locally as a writer, an archivist and an activist. Her work appears in the anthologies *The Other Woman: Women of Colour in Contemporary Canadian Literature; Another Way to Dance; Millenium Messages; Hot and Bothered;* and *Kitchen Talk.* Wong received the 1997 Asian Canadian Writers' Workshop Emerging Writer Award.

Press Gang Publishers has been producing vital and provocative books by women since 1975. Look for Press Gang titles at good bookstores everywhere.

POETRY HIGHLIGHTS

BY NATIVE AMERICAN WRITER CHRYSTOS:

Not Vanishing ISBN 0-88974-015-1. Over 10,000 copies sold.

In Her I Am ISBN 0-88974-033-x. Special collection of erotica.

Firepower ISBN 0-88974-047-x. Finalist, 1995 Lambda Literary Award for Poetry.

BY MÉTIS WRITER JOANNE ARNOTT:

Wiles of Girlhood ISBN 0-88974-034-8. Winner of the Gerald Lampert Award for best first book of poetry.

My Grass Cradle ISBN 0-88974-048-8. Poems that sing a triumph of the spirit.

BY POET AND NOVELIST CATHY STONEHOUSE:

The Words I Know ISBN 0-88974-037-2. A book to cherish for its insight, subtle crafting and naked courage.

OTHER HIGHLIGHTS

When Fox Is a Thousand BY LARISSA LAI ISBN 0-88974-041-0. Shortlisted for the 1996 Chapters/Books in Canada First Novel Award.

Bellydancer BY SKY LEE ISBN 0-88974-039-9. A collection of short fiction by the award-winning author of *Disappearing Moon Cafe*.

Prozac Highway BY PERSIMMON BLACKBRIDGE ISBN 0-88974-078-X. A 1998 Lambda Literary Award finalist for lesbian fiction.

Write for a free catalogue of all our books in print: Press Gang Publishers, 1723 Grant Street, Vancouver, B.C. v5L 2y6 Canada. http://www.pressgang.bc.ca